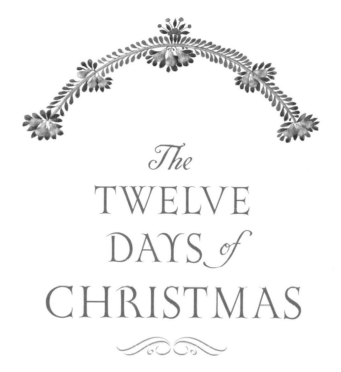

The
TWELVE
DAYS *of*
CHRISTMAS

The TWELVE DAYS *of* CHRISTMAS

ILLUSTRATED

by

GENNADY SPIRIN

MARSHALL CAVENDISH
CHILDREN

ON THE FIRST DAY OF CHRISTMAS
MY TRUE LOVE SENT TO ME:

A Partridge in a Pear Tree.

ON THE SECOND DAY OF CHRISTMAS
MY TRUE LOVE SENT TO ME:

Two Turtle Doves,

and a Partridge in a Pear Tree.

On the third day of Christmas
my true love sent to me:

Three French Hens,

Two Turtle Doves,

and a Partridge in a Pear Tree.

On the fourth day of Christmas
my true love sent to me:

Four Calling Birds,

Three French Hens,

Two Turtle Doves,

and a Partridge in a Pear Tree.

ON THE FIFTH DAY OF CHRISTMAS
MY TRUE LOVE SENT TO ME:

Five Golden Rings,

Four Calling Birds,

Three French Hens,

Two Turtle Doves,

and a Partridge in a Pear Tree.

On the sixth day of Christmas
my true love sent to me:

Six Geese-a-Laying,

Five Golden Rings,

Four Calling Birds,

Three French Hens,

Two Turtle Doves,

and a Partridge in a Pear Tree.

ON THE SEVENTH DAY OF CHRISTMAS
MY TRUE LOVE SENT TO ME:

Seven Swans-a-Swimming,

Six Geese-a-Laying,

Five Golden Rings,

Four Calling Birds,

Three French Hens,

Two Turtle Doves,

and a Partridge in a Pear Tree.

On the eighth day of Christmas
my true love sent to me:

Eight Maids-a-Milking,

Seven Swans-a-Swimming,

Six Geese-a-Laying,

Five Golden Rings,

Four Calling Birds,

Three French Hens,

Two Turtle Doves,

and a Partridge in a Pear Tree.

On the ninth day of Christmas
my true love sent to me:

Nine Ladies Dancing,

Eight Maids-a-Milking,

Seven Swans-a-Swimming,

Six Geese-a-Laying,

Five Golden Rings,

Four Calling Birds,

Three French Hens,

Two Turtle Doves,

and a Partridge in a Pear Tree.

ON THE TENTH DAY OF CHRISTMAS
MY TRUE LOVE SENT TO ME:

Ten Lords-a-Leaping,

Nine Ladies Dancing,

Eight Maids-a-Milking,

Seven Swans-a-Swimming,

Six Geese-a-Laying,

Five Golden Rings,

Four Calling Birds,

Three French Hens,

Two Turtle Doves,

and a Partridge in a Pear Tree.

On the eleventh day of Christmas
my true love sent to me:

Eleven Pipers Piping,

Ten Lords-a-Leaping,

Nine Ladies Dancing,

Eight Maids-a-Milking,

Seven Swans-a-Swimming,

Six Geese-a-Laying,

Five Golden Rings,

Four Calling Birds,

Three French Hens,

Two Turtle Doves,

and a Partridge in a Pear Tree.

ON THE TWELFTH DAY OF CHRISTMAS
MY TRUE LOVE SENT TO ME:

Twelve Drummers Drumming,
Eleven Pipers Piping,
Ten Lords-a-Leaping,
Nine Ladies Dancing,
Eight Maids-a-Milking,
Seven Swans-a-Swimming,
Six Geese-a-Laying,
Five Golden Rings,
Four Calling Birds,
Three French Hens,
Two Turtle Doves,
and a Partridge in a Pear Tree.

The TWELVE DAYS of CHRISTMAS

On the first day of Christ - mas my true love sent to me: A Par - tridge_ in a Pear Tree. On the

sec - ond day of Christ - mas my true love sent to me: Two Tur - tle Doves, and a Par - tridge_ in a Pear

Tree. On the third day of Christ - mas my true love sent to me: Three French Hens, Two Tur - tle Doves, and a

Par - tridge_ in a Pear Tree. On the fourth day of Christ - mas my true love sent to me:

Four Call - ing Birds, Three French_ Hens, Two Tur - tle Doves, and a Par - tridge_ in a Pear

Tree.   On the fifth day of Christ-mas my true love sent to me: Five   Gold-en   Rings,

Four __ Call-ing Birds,   Three French Hens,   Two __ Tur-tle Doves, and a   Par-tridge__ in a Pear

Repeat through no. 12, adding one line each repetition

Tree.   On the sixth day of Christ-mas my   true love sent to   me:
seventh day etc. . . .

6. Six   Geese a - Lay - ing,
7. Seven   Swans a - Swim - ming,
8. Eight   Maids a - Milk - ing,
9. Nine   La - dies Danc - ing,
10. Ten   Lords a - Leap - ing,
11. Eleven Pip - ers Pip - ing,
12. Twelve Drum-mers Drum-ming,

Five   Gold en   Rings, _____   Four __ Call - ing Birds,   Three French   Hens,

Through 11th day repeat. | *Final ending after 12th day.*

Two __ Tur - tle Doves, and a   Par - tridge__ in a Pear   Tree. _____   On the   Tree.

A NOTE ABOUT THE SONG'S ORIGINS

The song is associated with the twelve days of Christmas that stretch from Christmas Day, December 25, to Epiphany, January 6, when the three kings' visit to baby Jesus is celebrated.

No one knows the exact origins of "The Twelve Days of Christmas." The earliest version appears in a book called *Mirth without Mischief*, published in the early 1780s in England. The song is described as a "memory and forfeits game" played by children. A leader sings the first verse, a second child repeats the first verse and adds the second, a third child repeats the first two verses and adds a third, and so on, until a child forgets one of the verses that has been sung previously. He or she is then punished by being made to give up small change to the other players or to kiss them on the cheek.

Some Catholics have suggested that the song was written between 1558 and 1829, when Catholics in England were forbidden to practice their faith. The Catholics believed the song had hidden Christian meanings: "My true love" was God, the partridge was Jesus, the two turtle doves were the Old and New Testaments, and so on. Oppressed Catholics sang the song to show their depth of faith, assuming that their enemies would not understand the song's hidden Christian meanings.

Most scholars believe that the song originated in France, however, since the partridge wasn't introduced to England until the 1770s.

In some early versions, the "calling birds" were written as "collie birds," or blackbirds, and the five golden rings were meant to be five ring-necked birds such as pheasants. But over the centuries, the words have changed, and now "calling birds" is widely accepted and the rings are the kind you wear on your fingers.

Regardless of the various theories about the song's origins, people continue to sing it at Christmastime with great enthusiasm.

Gennady Spirin

In memory of my mother
—G.S.

LIBRARY OF CONGRESS CATALOGING-IN-PUBLICATION DATA
Twelve days of Christmas (English folk song)
The twelve days of Christmas / illustrated by Gennady Spirin.
p. cm.
Summary: On each of the twelve days of Christmas,
unusual and fanciful gifts arrive to celebrate the season.
ISBN 978-0-7614-5551-6
1. Folk songs, English—England—Texts. 2. Christmas music—Texts.
[1. Folk songs—England. 2. Christmas music] I. Spirin, Gennadii, ill. II. Title.
PZ8.3.T8517 2009
782.42'1723'0268—dc22
2008006476

The illustrations are rendered in watercolor and colored pencil.
Book design by Michael Nelson
Editor: Margery Cuyler

Printed in China
First edition
1 3 5 6 4 2

mc Marshall Cavendish
Children